PREHISTORIC ANIMALS

HOLIDAY HOUSE · NEW YORK

PREHISTORIC ANIMALS

BY GAIL GIBBONS

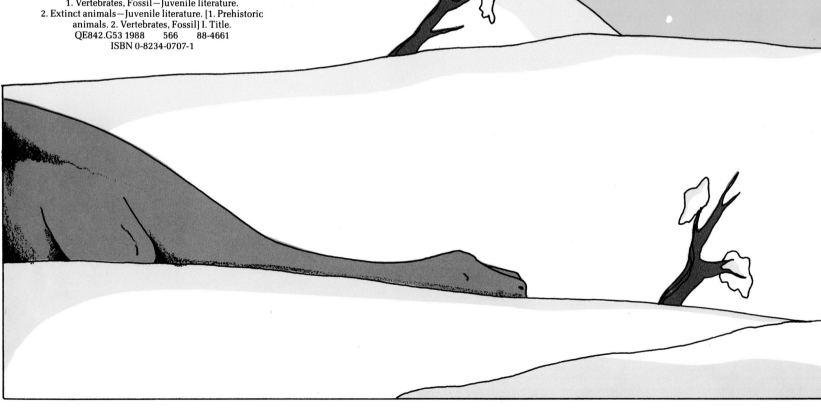

Special thanks to The American Museum of
Natural History, New York City

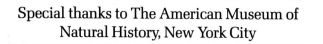

Copyright © 1988 by Gail Gibbons
All rights reserved
Printed in the United States of America
First Edition

Library of Congress Cataloging-in-Publication Data

Gibbons, Gail.
Prehistoric animals.

SUMMARY: Introduces, in text and illustrations, a
variety of prehistoric animals whose fossilized remains
have provided scientists with clues about their physical
characteristics and the environment in which they lived.
1. Vertebrates, Fossil—Juvenile literature.
2. Extinct animals—Juvenile literature. [1. Prehistoric
animals. 2. Vertebrates, Fossil] I. Title.
QE842.G53 1988   566   88-4661
ISBN 0-8234-0707-1

Millions of years ago
dinosaurs vanished from the earth.

Other prehistoric animals
continued to live.
Some were small.

Some were big.

Some were giant beasts.

Paleontologists know, from studying fossils, that the areas where these creatures lived slowly changed over millions of years. The animals changed, too.

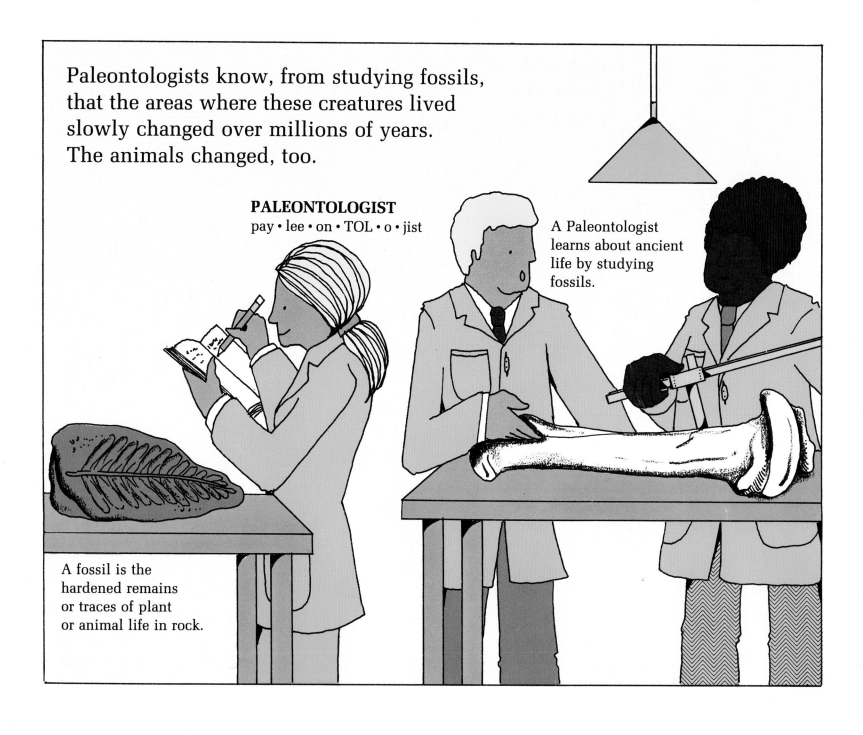

PALEONTOLOGIST
pay • lee • on • TOL • o • jist

A Paleontologist learns about ancient life by studying fossils.

A fossil is the hardened remains or traces of plant or animal life in rock.

Many prehistoric animals were plant eaters. Eohippus was a prehistoric animal about 12 inches high. It was the first horse and ate small, soft plants.

EOHIPPUS
e · o · HIP · us

Some prehistoric animals had horns. Brontotherium had a forked horn on the end of its nose for protection. It ate soft fruits and leaves. Unitatherium had three pairs of rounded horns. It ate tree leaves.

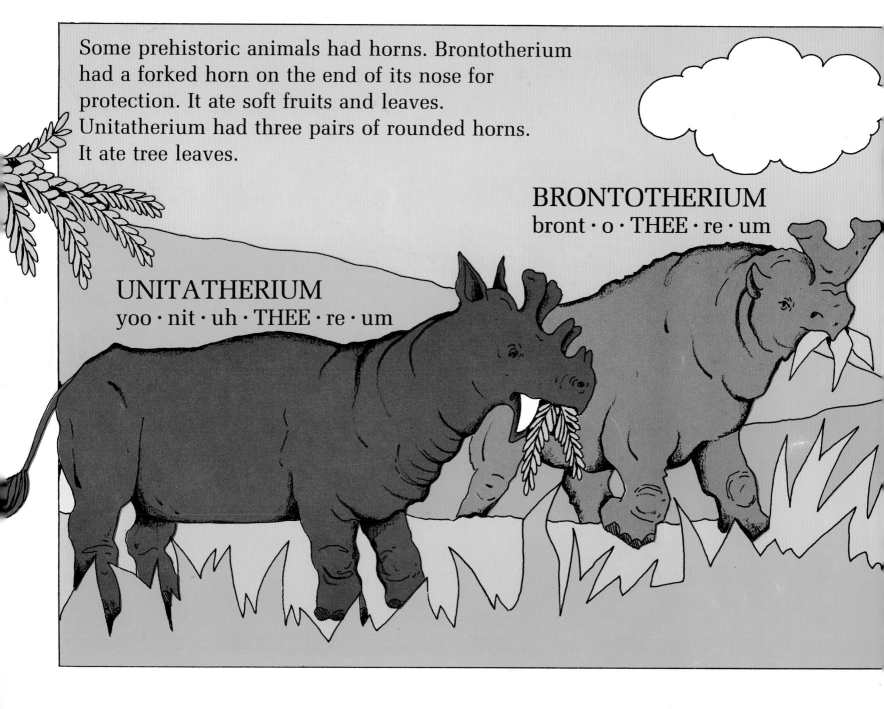

BRONTOTHERIUM
bront · o · THEE · re · um

UNITATHERIUM
yoo · nit · uh · THEE · re · um

Arsinoitherium was about 13 feet long and had long sharp horns to protect itself. It had strong legs and wide feet to support its weight. It was a plant eater, too.

ARSINOITHERIUM
r · sin · o · THEE · re · um

Barylambda was about eight feet long.
It had big legs and a fat tail.

BARYLAMBDA
bare · uh · LAM · da

ALTICAMELUS
alt · e · CAM · el · us

One of the first camels was Alticamelus. It was
about 11 feet tall and ate tree leaves.

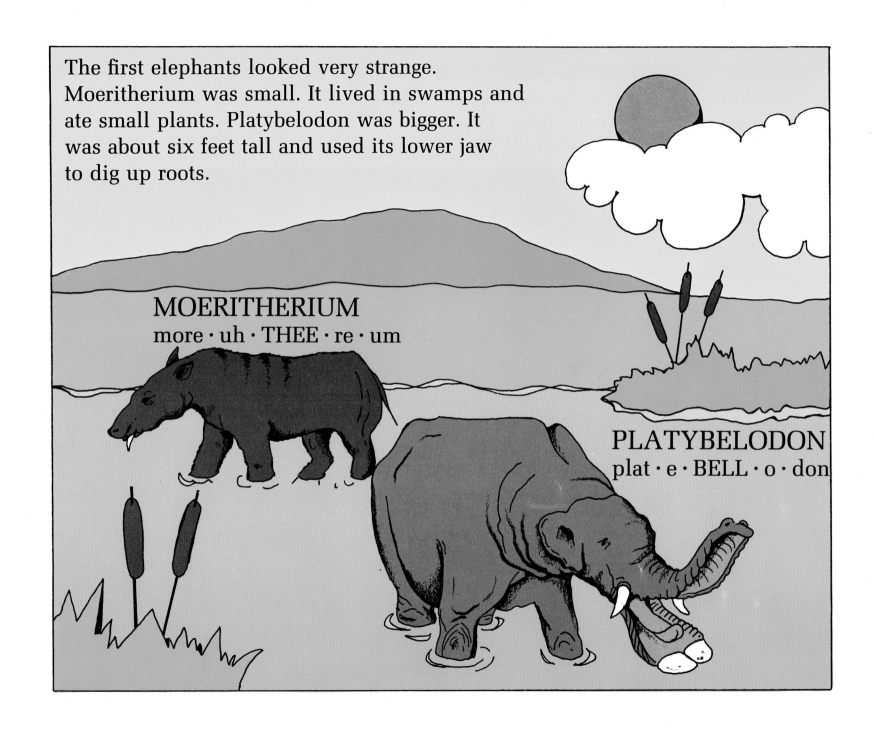

The first elephants looked very strange. Moeritherium was small. It lived in swamps and ate small plants. Platybelodon was bigger. It was about six feet tall and used its lower jaw to dig up roots.

MOERITHERIUM
more · uh · THEE · re · um

PLATYBELODON
plat · e · BELL · o · don

Later, the Mastadon and the Mammoth took the place of the earlier elephants. They were much bigger and ate twigs and leaves.

WOOLLY MAMMOTH
WOOL · e MAM · oth

MAMMOTH
MAM · oth

MASTADON
MASS · ta · don

MOROPUS
more · OPP · us

Moropus was a plant eater, too. It looked very
strange and had long claws.

MEGATHERIUM
meg · uh · THEE · re · um

Megatherium was very big. It stood about 20 feet tall and had huge claws, too.

The biggest prehistoric animal was
Baluchitherium. It was 23 feet tall!
Baluchitherium nibbled leaves
from tall trees.

BALUCHITHERIUM
ba · luch · uh · THEE · re · um

Some prehistoric animals were meat eaters. Glyptodon was about nine feet long and was covered with bony armour for protection. It ate worms and bugs.

GLYPTODON
GLIP · toe · don

There were prehistoric animals that looked like big pigs. Dinohyus was about as big as a cow. It ate the meat of dead animals.

DINOHYUS
dine · uh · HI · us

Diatryma was about six feet tall. This bird's wings were too small for it to fly. It attacked and ate smaller animals.

DIATRYMA
die · uh · TRY · ma

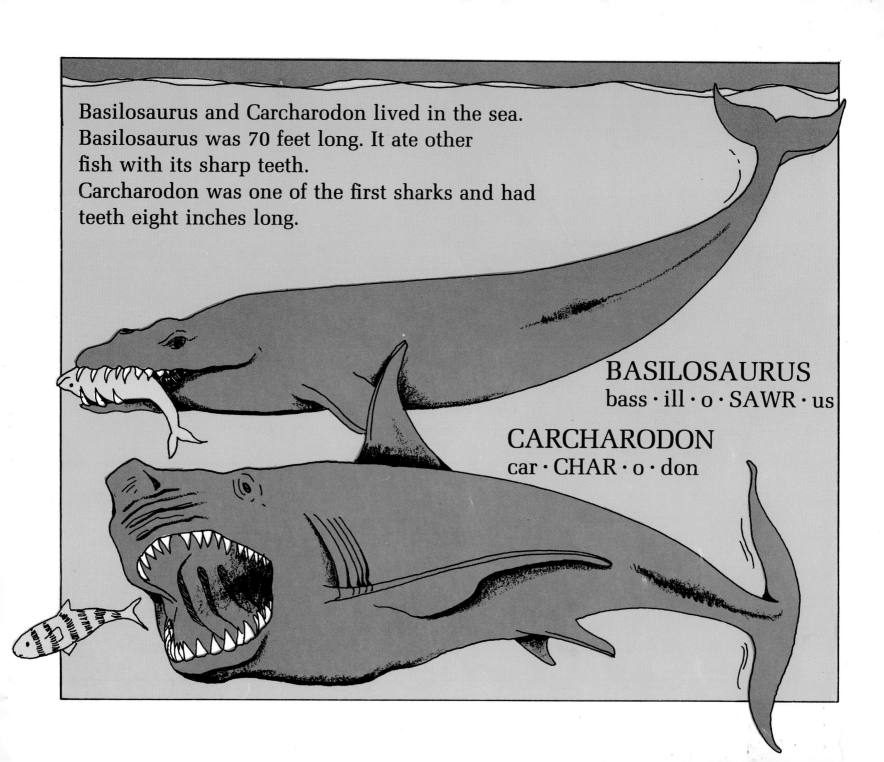

Basilosaurus and Carcharodon lived in the sea.
Basilosaurus was 70 feet long. It ate other
fish with its sharp teeth.
Carcharodon was one of the first sharks and had
teeth eight inches long.

BASILOSAURUS
bass · ill · o · SAWR · us

CARCHARODON
car · CHAR · o · don

Smilodon, a saber-toothed cat, had long, curved, sharp teeth. It weighed as much as 600 pounds. Dire wolves hunted in packs. They looked very much like today's wolves.

SMILODON
SMILE · o · don

DIRE WOLF
DIE · er WOLF

The most fierce looking of all the prehistoric
animals were Andrewsarchus and Megistotherium.
Andrewsarchus had many rounded teeth and ate
almost anything.

ANDREWSARCHUS
an · drew · SAR · kus

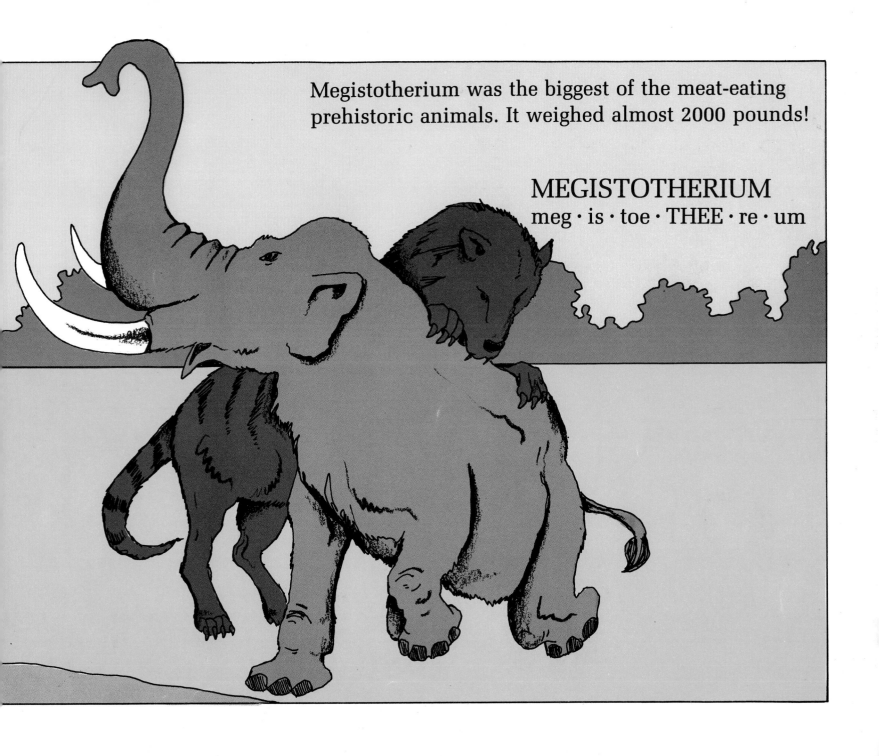

Megistotherium was the biggest of the meat-eating prehistoric animals. It weighed almost 2000 pounds!

MEGISTOTHERIUM
meg · is · toe · THEE · re · um

Most prehistoric animals were
strange looking creatures.

The world and the animals living in it
are always slowly changing.

WHEN THE PREHISTORIC ANIMALS LIVED

65 million years ago

MOERITHERIUM
BASILOSAURUS

ARSINOITHERIUM
BALUCHITHERIUM

BARYLAMBDA

ANDREWSARCHUS
UNITATHERIUM
EOHIPPUS
DIATRYMA
CARCHARODON

BRONTOTHERIUM

54 million years ago

38 million years ago

26 million years ago

MOROPUS
BALUCHITHERIUM

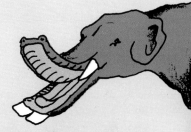

PLATYBELODON
DINOHYUS

ALTICAMELUS

PLATYBELODON
GLYPTODON

WOOLLY
MAMMOTH
SMILODON
MEGATHERIUM
DIRE WOLF
MASTADON
MAMMOTH

MEGISTOTHERIUM

7 million years ago ▶ **2 million years ago** ▶ **10 thousand years ago** ▶

SOME CREATURES THAT LIVED WITH THE PREHISTORIC ANIMALS MILLIONS OF YEARS AGO STILL LIVE TODAY.

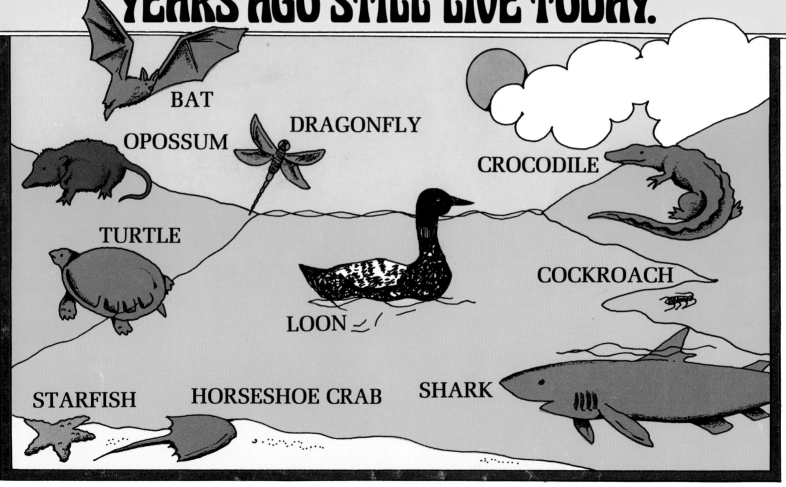

BAT

OPOSSUM

DRAGONFLY

CROCODILE

TURTLE

COCKROACH

LOON

STARFISH   HORSESHOE CRAB   SHARK

Date Due

FEB 11 1989		
MAR 9 1989		
MAR 16 1989		
APR 6 1989		
MAY 18 1989		
JUL 6 1989		
AUG 20 1989		

E566   Gibbons, Gail
AUTHOR

GIB   Prehistoric animals
TITLE